Hot Henrietta and l

Henrietta longs to have gla
like her father's secretary, Jeanny, but however hard
she tries, she just can't stop nibbling them away.
Then her father offers her the reward of a lovely ring
if she can grow ten perfect nails, and that makes a
big difference!

From hypnosis to wearing gloves, Henrietta tries
every possible cure in spite of her brother Hank's
continuous teasing. Can she succeed, or is she
doomed to be a life-long nibbler? The answer lies in
this very funny book, which is the third about the
Lawes family. The other titles, also in Puffin, are
Hank Prank and Hot Henrietta and *Hank Prank in
Love*.

Other books by Jules Older

HANK PRANK AND HOT HENRIETTA
HANK PRANK IN LOVE

Jules and Effin Older

Hot Henrietta and Nailbiters United

illustrated
by Lisa Kopper

PUFFIN BOOKS

PUFFIN BOOKS

Published by the Penguin Group
27 Wrights Lane, London W8 5TZ, England
Viking Penguin Inc., 40 West 23rd Street, New York, New York 10010, USA
Penguin Books Australia Ltd, Ringwood, Victoria, Australia
Penguin Books Canada Ltd, 2801 John Street, Markham, Ontario, Canada L3R 1B4
Penguin Books (NZ) Ltd, 182–190 Wairau Road, Auckland 10, New Zealand

Penguin Books Ltd, Registered Offices: Harmondsworth, Middlesex, England

First published by William Heinemann Ltd 1987
Published in Puffin Books 1989
3 5 7 9 10 8 6 4 2

Printed and bound in Great Britain by
Cox & Wyman Ltd, Reading
Filmset in Palatino

Contents

To the
Future
Ex-Nailbiters
of the World
and to
Barbara Larson
too.

Glammer Nails

"I'll get it! I'll get it!" Henrietta beat Hank to the phone and made a face at him as she listened to the voice at the other end.

"Good morning, Henrietta. This is Jeanny." Jeanny was the receptionist at the office where Henrietta's father worked. She used to babysit for Hank and Henrietta when they were little.

"Hi, Jeanny. Are you at work?"

"Yes, Love. I'm glad I caught you before you left for school. Can you come down to the office this afternoon? I have something to show you."

"What is it, Jeanny?"

"Never mind what it is. Just come down and have a look."

"Oh, Jeanny, give me a hint. Go on. Pleee aaazzze. Just a little hint."

"Well...O.K. It's something to do with my hands."

Henrietta thought for a moment. "It's a

ring! An engagement ring! You're engaged, Jeanny!"

Jeanny laughed. "No, it's not that, but it's something pretty exciting. In fact, it's something *very* exciting."

After school Henrietta raced down to Jeanny's office. Jeanny was talking on the telephone when Henrietta walked in. She smiled and held up one finger. Henrietta nodded and smiled back. As soon as she put the phone down, Jeanny twirled round in her chair and placed both hands on the desk in front of her. She spread her fingers wide. "Well?"

Henrietta looked puzzled. "Well, what?"

"Look!"

"I *am* looking! You don't have a new ring, and, let's see...one, two, three... you've got all ten fingers. What am I supposed to be looking for?"

"Have a *good* look, Henrietta. Don't you see anything new?"

"No, I...oh, Jeanny! Your nails! You've got fingernails!"

Jeanny's nails were deep red, perfectly rounded, and they stuck out nearly half an inch from her fingertips. "Aren't they beautiful?"

"But Jeanny, yesterday your nails looked as bad as mine." Henrietta glanced down at her own little hands. They were not a pretty sight.

Henrietta was a nailbiter. She ate nails for breakfast, she ate nails for lunch, she ate nails for supper. She had nail snacks and nail desserts. She bit her nails in the morning when she got up and she nibbled them at night when she went to bed. Sometimes she wondered if she ate nails in her sleep!

But as bad as Henrietta was, Jeanny was worse. At least Henrietta had half-nails. Jeanny had none. That is, until

3

today. Today, she had the most perfect fingernails Henrietta had ever seen.

"How did you grow your nails so fast, Jeanny?"

Jeanny laughed and motioned for Henrietta to come closer. "I'll let you in on a little secret, Love. I didn't actually grow them. I bought them."

"You mean there's a fingernail shop?"

"Yep."

"And you can buy *real* fingernails?"

"Well, they're not real nails. They're Glamour Nails. They're made of silicone." She tapped them on the desk. They sounded like real nails. "They're so strong, even *I* can't bite them. If I bite them, I'll chip my teeth, not the nails. You can't burn them, and you can't break them with a hammer."

"Wow!" Henrietta yelled. "They're just what I need. Can I try one on?"

"They're stuck on, and they're impossible to get off. I've got Glamour Nails for life!"

"Oh Jeanny, you're so lucky. Do you think I could get some too?"

"Why not? In fact, why don't you ask your father right now. He's in his office."

Henrietta marched into his room.

"Hi Henrietta. How about a hug?"

"Hi Dad. Here's a hug. How about some Glamour Nails?"

"Some what?"

"Glamour Nails. Like Jeanny's."

"Oh yes, she showed me. I wondered how long it would be before you'd want some."

"I want some *now!*"

"What a surprise!"

"Well, can I have some?"

"Nope."

Nope? Henrietta expected a "Yep", not a "Nope".

"You mean 'Yep', don't you, Dad?"

"Nope, I mean Nope."

Henrietta's temper simmered. "Why can't I have Glamour Nails?"

"Because —"

Henrietta's temper bubbled. "Because why?"

"Because —"

Henrietta's temper boiled over. "Because you don't want me to have beautiful nails! Because you want me to go around with bit-off nails all my life! Because —"

"Because, Henrietta, Glamour Nails cost £65 a set."

"Oh," said Henrietta in a post-temper, cool-down, quiet sort of voice.

"But I've had another idea. Maybe the reason you bite your nails is that you haven't had an incentive not to."

"What's an incentive?"

"An incentive is...an incentive is...a good reason to do something. Or a good reason *not* to do something. For example, you have an incentive not to lose your temper because, if you do, you may also lose your bike for a week. Do you see what I mean?"

"Yeah, I see what you mean. But since you won't let me have Glamour Nails, what incentive do I have to stop biting my nails?"

"Well, I was just thinking about the ring you saw last week..."

"What ring?"

"The one in the magazine."

Henrietta suddenly remembered. The ad said,

SPECIAL
NEVER TO BE REPEATED OFFER!!

and it showed a picture of a silver ring with three black stones for only £5.99.

6

She'd left a copy of the ad on her parents'
bed with the part that read,

DON'T DELAY! ORDER TODAY!
SAVE! SAVE! SAVE!

circled three times in red ink.

"Oooh, that ring! I'd love that ring!"
Henrietta was so excited that she bit her
fingernail.

Her father said, "Ahem."

Henrietta whipped her fingernail out of

her mouth and clenched her fists. "Help! What am I doing?"

"You appear to be biting your nails, Henrietta."

"See? I do it without thinking, Dad. How can I stop when I don't even know when I'm starting?"

"It won't be easy, but now you've got an incentive. Mom and I will buy you that ring if you stop biting your nails. The day you get ten out of ten, the ring is yours."

"Ten outta' ten? You mean, I have to have ten perfect nails before I get the ring?"

"That's how many nails you have, Henrietta."

"How about half of 'em? How about five?"

"Ten nails you have, and ten nails you must grow."

"How am I going to do it? How am I ever going to do it?"

* * *

Henrietta asked herself the same question that night in bed. She'd had lots of practice in nailbiting, but she'd had almost no practice in *not* nailbiting. Or

8

was it nail *not*-biting? Either way, she didn't know how she was ever going to get ten out of ten, even with an incentive.

Henrietta reached for a pencil and pad from the drawer beside her bed. She thought for a few minutes. Then she wrote:

How To Stop Biting Nails
  by Henrietta Lawes
1. Glammer Nails (too expensive)
2.

"No Glamour Nails for me," muttered Henrietta. "And no ring if I don't stop munching my fingernails. But how can I stop? They taste so good!"

She slipped the pad back into the drawer, turned out the light, snuggled under the covers, bit her nails, and went to sleep.

Hypmosis

Several days later at breakfast, Henrietta said to her father, "Dad, I want you to hypmotize me."

"Pardon?"

"I said I want you to hypmotize me."

"That's what I thought you said." Mr. Lawes spread raspberry jam on his toast and took a bite. "Mmmmmm, lovely new jam. Have you tried it?"

"*Da-ad!*"

"Oh yes, Henrietta. You were asking about hyp -*no* -sis. Now why do you want to be hyp -*no* -tized?"

"So I can stop biting my nails."

"What makes you think hypnosis would do the trick?"

"Because on television I saw a man hypmo — hyp -*no* -tize a whole lot of people. He just made them go to sleep, and then they did whatever he told them."

"That's right," said Hank. "I saw it too. Looked dead easy."

"So how about it, Dad? Will you do it?"

"Sorry, Henrietta. I —"

Henrietta's temper didn't wait for her Dad to finish his sentence.

"Why not? Why won't you?"

"Because —"

"Because you don't care if I have horrible nails, that's why! You don't bite your nails, so you think I can just stop biting mine anytime. And besides, you don't want to buy me that ring, do you?"

"Henrietta!" said her father sharply. "Henrietta. If you will tuck that temper of yours into your back pocket for a minute and let me finish...the reason I won't hypnotize you is that I don't know *how* to hypnotize you."

"Oh," said Henrietta in a quiet voice. That was a reason she hadn't thought of. But it wasn't a good enough reason for a desperate, hot-tempered nailbiter. "It's so easy. I could show you how to do it. Even Hank could show you how to do it!"

"What do you mean, 'even Hank'," snarled her brother.

"Oh, you know what I mean, Hank."

Mrs. Lawes put down the newspaper

11

she had been trying to read. "Look Henrietta, I think you should drop the idea of hypnosis. Your father doesn't know how. Hank *certainly* doesn't know how. And I think when you really decide you want to stop biting your nails, you'll stop all by yourself...like I did."

Three pairs of eyes suddenly shot in the direction of Mrs. Lawes.

"You mean...?"

"You mean...?"

"You mean...?"

"That's right," Mrs. Lawes smiled. "I'm an ex-nailbiter!"

"Mom, you never told me! How did you stop?"

"It wasn't easy. And I was the world's worst biter when I was your age. I didn't stop until I went away to college. One day an incentive came along." Mrs. Lawes winked at Mr. Lawes.

Henrietta fidgeted in her chair. "Well ...tell me. What was the incentive?"

"The incentive was a 'who' not a 'what'."

"What?" repeated Henrietta.

"Not 'what', 'who'," teased Hank. He had seen his mother wink.

Henrietta was still confused. "If someone doesn't tell me what's going on..."

"I fell in love...with your father," said Mrs. Lawes. "I decided there and then to stop biting my nails. And I never bit them again."

"That's it, Henrietta!" laughed Hank. "Fall in love. You'd LOVVVE to fall in love, wouldn't you, Henrietta? I'd like to see the guy who's brave enough to fall in love with you!"

"How would you like to see stars, Hank!" Henrietta was in no mood for teasing.

That night, when Henrietta was on her way to bed, a voice hissed at her from Hank's room. "Psssst. Henrietta. Come here."

It was Hank. "Come in — and close the door." It was so dark, Henrietta could hardly see the bed. In fact, she could hardly see Hank.

"What are you doing, Hank? Why is your desk light under your desk?"

"I want to show you something," he whispered.

"Hank, there's no one in here but me. You don't have to whisper."

"Shhhhh. Be quiet or you'll break my concentration."

Hank sat on the floor at the foot of his bed. Around his head, he'd wrapped a bath mat. It was supposed to look like a turban. It didn't. It looked like a bath mat.

"Hank, why have you got that ridiculous bath. . .?"

"Shhhh. Sit down, Henrietta. Right here, in front of me."

Henrietta sat down.

"Now cross your legs. Like mine."

Henrietta crossed her legs.

"Now stop grinning and do as I say."

Henrietta stopped grinning.

From behind his back, Hank pulled an old, gold pocket watch. A string was tied

to the watch. He dangled the watch in front of Henrietta's face. "See this watch, Henrietta? With the help of this watch, I, Hank Prank, am about to cure you of nailbiting through my powers of hypmosis."

"Hyp -*no* -sis, Dummy," muttered Henrietta.

"Do you want to be cured or not? Now be quiet!"

Again Hank dangled the watch in front of Henrietta's face. Then he gave it a push. It slowly swung back and forth, back and forth before Henrietta's eyes. "Watch the watch, Henrietta. Watch the watch." Hank spoke in a deep, slow voice. "Soon you will get sleepy. Very sleepy. Soon you will get ver-ry, ver-ry sleeeepy."

Henrietta watched the watch. Henrietta listened to Hank's voice. It was getting lower and lower and slower and slower.

"Your eyelids are getting heavy. Ver-ry heavy. Ver-ry heavvvvyyy. You are going to sleeeep. You are sound asleeeeep. When you awake you will never again bite your nails. Never, never again. But now you must sleep... sleeeep... sleeeeeep... sleeeeeeep...sleee..."

Henrietta was just about to close her eyes when suddenly...the watch clunked to the floor. Hank's bath-matted head s-l-o-w-l-y began tilting to the left. Like a torpedoed ship, Hank listed further and further to port. Ever so s-l-o-w-l-y, Hank sank into a heap on the floor, sounnnnnd asleeeeeep. And snoring.

Henrietta looked at Hank. She shook her head. She got up and tiptoed out of the room. "Some hypnotizer," she muttered. "Hyp -snor- tizer, more like it."

* * *

When Henrietta hopped into her own bed, more wide awake than she'd been all day, she pulled out her list and did some crossing-out and writing-in. Here's what the new, post-hypnosis list looked like:

How To Stop Biting Nails
      by Henrietta Lawes
1. Glammer Nails (too expensive)
2. Hypnosis (doesn't work)
3.

She read the list out loud, turned off the light, thought about how silly Hank looked with his head wrapped up in a bath mat, snuggled under the covers, bit her nails, and finally fell asleep.

Hot Stuff

"That's it! That's it!" shouted Henrietta. "I've found the answer!"

"To what?" Hank asked.

"To my problem."

"*Which* problem?"

Henrietta narrowed her eyes and looked straight at Hank. "Besides having you as a brother, Hank, my *only* problem is nailbiting. And I've just found the answer."

"Have you tried hypnosis?"

Henrietta threw her slipper at Hank and raced out of the room carrying the magazine she was reading. "Mom! Mom! Listen to this!"

Mrs. Lawes looked up from her book. "What is it? Wait — let me guess. Another never-to-be-repeated special offer?"

"Well, sort of. But this is serious, Mom. Listen!"

"Now you, too, can have long, beautiful
nails with new
NO FAIL NAILS.
Just brush it on.
It looks like ordinary polish.
It smells like ordinary polish.
But it doesn't taste like ordinary polish.
It's HOT! HOT! HOT!
Guaranteed no more biting with new
NO FAIL NAILS."

"Can I get some, Mom? Please?"
"Well, I suppose it wouldn't hurt to
try."
That afternoon Henrietta was waiting at
the door when her mother returned home
with the shopping. "Here's your NO
FAIL NAILS, Henrietta. The sales girl
who sold it to me said it cured her. And
I must say, she did have beautiful nails."
Henrietta bounded up the stairs to her
room. She shut the door behind her and
ripped open the bag. Inside was a bottle
of bright red nail polish. The label read,

NO FAIL NAILS
The polish that's
Too Hot to Bite

19

Henrietta couldn't wait to try NO FAIL NAILS. She twisted open the cap and carefully painted each of her raggedy half-nails with the fiery, red polish. Then she held up her hands and gazed at each nail. She imagined how they'd look in a few weeks' time. They'd be just as beautiful as Jeanny's Glamour Nails — long, red, and absolutely perfect. And on her right hand there'd be that shiny silver ring. Henrietta was so excited, she bit her nails.

"YOWIE ZOWIE, DAVID BOWIE!!! Hey, this stuff is hot!"

Henrietta ran her tongue along her lips. "Yikes, it's hotter and hotter! Dragon juice!" she yelped. "It's dragon juice!" She leapt up and down and flicked her tongue in and out like a snake. "WOW!!!!"

That night at dinner, Hank was the first to notice. "Hey Henrietta! Your fingers

20

are bleeding. Quick! Somebody get the doctor!"

"I'll doctor *you*, Hank, if you don't..."

Mr. Lawes interrupted his daughter in mid-threat. "Hold on a minute, you two. Hank, cut the wise-cracks. Henrietta, what *have* you done to your nails?"

"I've painted them with NO FAIL NAILS to help me stop biting them."

"What's NO FAIL NAILS?"

"It's a special polish."

Hank laughed loudly. "It would have to be *very* special to keep you from gnawing through it. Is it made of steel, Henrietta?"

"For your information, Hank, it looks like ordinary polish, and it smells like ordinary polish, but it..."

"Bet it *is* ordinary polish. Bet it's just a trick."

"You're wrong, Hank. It's very..."

Suddenly Henrietta stopped talking. Suddenly, Henrietta did something Mr. Lawes and Mrs. Lawes and Hank Lawes had rarely seen her do. She turned to her brother and with a big, sweet smile, said, "Hank, dear, I think you're right. I bet it *is* just a trick. You try it, and if it is just ordinary polish, I'll take it right back to the shop."

"You mean you want me to put that silly looking stuff on my finger nails? And then bite them? You must be crazy!"

"You just need a little bit. And it'll wash right off."

Hank grumbled and muttered. "Well, all right. But I'll only do it as a scientific experiment to prove that I'm right and you're wrong!"

Henrietta pulled the bottle out of her pocket and handed it to Hank. He painted his thumbnail.

"Don't bite it until it's dry, Hank. Blow on it."

Hank blew. Then Hank bit.

Henrietta watched Hank.

Mr. Lawes watched Hank.

Mrs. Lawes watched Hank.

Hank smiled at them. "See? I told yooouoOOOWWWW!!!!"

Hank took off. He leapt out of his chair. He hopped around the room like a rabbit. He clutched his throat and yelped, "Yarrrrgggghhhh."

Hank twisted. He coughed. He spluttered. "I'm dying! I'm dying! Help!" Then, in one last dramatic gesture, he whirled round three times and crashed to the floor with legs and arms outstretched.

"Something wrong, Hank?" Henrietta asked sweetly.

Hank jerked a few times and then slowly got up. "Boy, you're right! That stuff is dynamite! If you bite your nails through that, Henrietta, you're crazier than I thought you were!"

"Told you it wasn't ordinary polish," smiled Henrietta.

That night, Henrietta took out her list. She filled in the space beside number 3. Now the list read:

How To Stop Biting Nails
by Henrietta Lawes
1. Glammer Nails (too expensive)
2. Hypnosis (doesn't work)
3. NO FAIL NAILS (Hot stuff!!!)

Henrietta didn't write number 4 on the list. She didn't need to. She had finally discovered how to stop biting her nails.

Before turning out her light, Henrietta looked at the bottle of polish once more. She looked at her own short, bright red nails. "Won't be long now," she thought. Then she smiled, crawled under the sheets and went to sleep.

Cool Down

"Morning, Henrietta," Hank grinned. Then he sang,
  "Did you make it through the night,
    Without a teeny-weeny bite?"
"I most certainly did," Henrietta replied. "And I should warn you, Hanky Panky, that when these nails are fully grown, I'll have ten very dangerous weapons. So watch your step!"
"Oohhhhh, scary."
Mr. Lawes sighed a long, loud sigh. "Kids, isn't it a bit early in the morning for all this?" He looked at Henrietta. "Congratulations, Henrietta. You've made a good start. Just take it one day at a time."
And today was Henrietta's first nail-free day — no nails for breakfast, no nails for lunch, and no nails for supper. "Hope I don't starve," she thought as she walked to school.

Henrietta made it through her reading lesson without a nibble.

Henrietta made it through her spelling lesson without a nibble.

Henrietta made it through lunch, she made it through art, and she made it through multiplication. All without a nibble.

It was time for the last lesson of the day — science. Henrietta took out her folder and opened it to the page on the cabbage moth. "We've been reading about the cabbage moth for weeks," she thought. "I'm bored, bored, bored with the rotten old cabbage moth."

Then Henrietta looked at her bright red fingernails. "They're not boring," she thought. "They're exciting! NO FAIL NAILS are wonderful!" She lovingly stroked each stubby little nail. "I wonder if the polish is still as hot as it was last night."

Henrietta tried to remember exactly how hot it was last night. Was it as hot as pepper? Was it as hot as chili? Was it as hot as curry? Henrietta couldn't remember.

"I'll just take another itsy-bitsy taste." Slowly, she raised her hand to her mouth. She took a little lick. It was still hot all right. But was it *as* hot?

She took another lick. Perhaps it wasn't quite as hot. Just one more lick and she'd know for sure.

She took another lick.

Then she took a nibble.

She took another nibble.

Then she took a bite.

She took another bite.

Then she...

Before she knew what she was doing, she licked and nibbled and bit through all ten fingers of NO FAIL NAILS!

*   *   *

That night Henrietta pulled out the list. Now it said:

How To Stop Biting Nails
    by Henrietta Lawes
1. Glammer Nails (too expensive)
2. Hypnosis (doesn't work)
3. NO FAIL NAILS (Hot stuff!!!)
   NO FAIL NAILS (failed - not hot enough)
4.

Henrietta read the list out loud, tossed the bottle of NO FAIL NAILS into her bottom drawer, turned out the light, crawled between the sheets, bit her nails, and went to sleep.

Gloves

"That's about all this box will hold," said Mrs. Lawes. "Some little girl will be very happy that you've outgrown so many clothes, Henrietta. Is there anything else we can squeeze in?"

"Just this old pair of woollen gloves, but the thumbs are full of holes." Henrietta held them up for her mother to see.

"Probably not worth keeping," said her mother. She closed the lid and stuck sticky tape across the top.

Henrietta tried on the gloves. Each finger was knitted in a different colour. "These were my favourite gloves. They're a bit small, but I hate to throw 'em away. Wish I could think of something to do with 'em."

Just then Hank appeared at Henrietta's bedroom door. "Whatcha' doin' with those gloves on, Henrietta? Don't you

want everyone to see your gorgeous NO
FAIL NAILS?"

Henrietta hissed.

Henrietta steamed.

Henrietta blew up! "If you so much as
mention NO FAIL NAILS once more,
Hank, just — once — more, I'll..."
Henrietta raised two brightly coloured,
clenched fists in front of Hank's face,
dangerously close to Hank's nose.

Luckily for Hank, their mother was still
in the room. "Break it up, you two. Hank,
that was a very unkind thing to say when
you know how hard your sister is trying
to stop biting her nails."

"Sorry," Hank mumbled.

"Bet you're *not* sorry," Henrietta grumbled.

"Henrietta! That's enough! Hank said he was sorry, and that's the end of it. Now take off those gloves and help me carry this box out to the front porch."

Henrietta took off one glove. She was pulling the last finger out of the other glove when, all of a sudden, she stopped. She looked straight at Hank and smiled a big toothy smile. "Hank, my dear sweet brother, you've just given me an idea."

Slowly, one finger at a time, Henrietta put the gloves back on.

"Wha...wha...what idea?" stuttered Hank. He remembered the last time Henrietta smiled at him like that.

"Don't worry, Hank, it won't hurt you... this time." Henrietta raised both gloved hands. "There. My hands shall remain covered until my nails are long and glamorous."

Hank's head jerked and his eyes blinked. "You mean you're *never* going to take 'em off, not even to eat or sleep?"

"Right. Not even to eat or sleep."

"Not even to go to school?"

"Not even to go to school."

Hank raised his eyebrows, shook his

31

head, and made a low whistling sound. "Whew. I've gotta' hand it to you, Henrietta. When you decide to do something, you *really* decide to do something."

After supper that night, it was Hank's turn to wash the dishes and Henrietta's turn to dry.

"Don't you think you should take off your gloves, Henrietta?" her father suggested. "We've already had one glass of spilt juice and a plate of peas on the floor tonight."

"Ah, come on, Dad, anyone could spill a little juice and a few peas. Don't worry, I'm getting used to these gloves. They're just like a second skin. In a couple of weeks, when my nails are all grown out, I won't need to..."

C-R-A-S-H!

Henrietta's father looked down at his feet. Henrietta looked down at her father's feet.

"Uh oh," Hank mumbled.

"What were you saying, Henrietta?" asked her father as he picked up the pieces of broken glass. "In a couple of weeks you won't need to what?"

Henrietta answered in a very soft voice. "I won't need to wear gloves any more."

"Well, let's hope we all survive until then."

*   *   *

When Henrietta crawled into bed that night, she felt sorry she'd spilt the juice and dropped the peas and broken the dish. But she felt happy she'd finally discovered a way to stop biting her nails.

She pulled out the list. It was growing longer and longer — just like she imagined her fingernails were growing longer and longer under her gloves. It said:

How To Stop Biting Nails
by Henrietta Lawes
1. Glammer Nails (too expensive)
2. Hypnosis (doesn't work)
3. NO FAIL NAILS (Hot stuff!!!)
   NO FAIL NAILS (failed -not hot enough)
4. Gloves (the answer??)

Henrietta turned off her light, pulled the covers up under her chin, felt her thumbs poking through the holes in her gloves, *did not bite her nails*, and went to sleep.

Snip! Snip! Snip!

When Henrietta woke up the next morning, her gloves were missing!

She looked on the bed.

She looked under the bed.

She looked under the blankets.

Finally, she found them tucked under her pillow. "Whew! What a relief! I could've eaten them in my sleep!"

She pulled the gloves back on, got dressed for school, and went down to breakfast.

"How do you think you'll manage at school with gloves on?" her father asked.

"Perfectly," Henrietta answered cooly. "My gloves are like my second skin."

Hank poked his head out from behind the cereal box. "You're crazy, Henrietta! You can't keep those gloves on all the time."

"Oh no? You just wait and see!"

Henrietta got to school just as the bell rang. She had hardly stepped inside the door before someone asked, "Why the gloves, Henrietta?"

In an it's-too-too-terrible-to-talk-about voice, Henrietta answered, "I have a condition on my hands. I have to wear gloves for about...uh...about two weeks until the condition is cured."

Henrietta's three best friends, Natalie, Sophie and Laura were sitting together at the art table. So was Henrietta's un-best friend, Kate. They all looked at Henrietta's gloves. They all looked at each other. They all looked at Henrietta.

"Is it catching?" Natalie asked.

"Is it sore?" Sophie asked.

"Can I see it?" Laura asked.

"No. No. No. And stop asking questions. You make me feel like I have some horrible disease."

Kate snickered. "But, Henrietta, if it *isn't* some horrible disease, why can't we see it?"

Henrietta felt her temper hotting up.

She felt her patience running out.

She felt her fuse burning short.

Henrietta's teacher, Mrs. Hayford, had seen Henrietta's temper in action before.

"I think your gloves are very pretty, Henrietta. Now why don't you help me pass round the paper for art."

Mrs. Hayford handed Henrietta a large stack of drawing paper. Because Henrietta's gloves were slippery, she had to hold the stack very tightly with both hands. Sophie, Natalie and Laura each took one piece of paper from the top of the stack. Then it was Kate's turn.

"I need three pieces, Henrietta," said Kate in her sweetest voice. And before Henrietta could stop her, Kate snatched three sheets of paper from the *bottom* of the stack.

"Hey! Wait a minute!" yelled Henrietta.

But it was too late. The whole stack of paper slid out of Henrietta's hands and slithered to the floor. "Now look what you've done, Kate!" cried Henrietta. "You did that on purpose, didn't you?"

Kate smiled sweetly and shook her head. "Tsk. Tsk. I don't know what you mean, Henrietta. But maybe if you took off those silly gloves..."

Henrietta's gloved hands curled up into gloved fists. There's no telling what would have happened if, just at that moment, Mrs. Hayford hadn't stepped in between Henrietta and Kate. But step in she did. "Never mind, Henrietta," she said. "We'll all help you pick it up."

When lunchtime arrived, Henrietta opened her lunch box and found a peanut butter and jam sandwich — her favourite. She took a big bite. As soon as her teeth sank in, peanut butter and jam squished out, all over her gloves. Thick, brown, peanut butter. Sticky, red jam.

Henrietta licked the peanut butter and jam off her thumbs. "Now, how am I going to get the rest off?"

She tried wiping it off with her hand-kerchief. The peanut butter stayed stuck.

She tried wiping it off with a piece of paper. The jam stayed stuck. "Oh well, I'll just have to lick it off!"

Henrietta stuck a woollen finger into her mouth and took a big lick. "Yuuuukkkk! Hairy peanut butter!"

Henrietta felt like throwing up. She spat out the peanut butter. She spat out the jam. She pulled hairy strands of wool off her tongue and out of her teeth.

"This is disgusting," Henrietta muttered. She put what was left of the sandwich back in her lunch box and pulled out an apple. "Guess I'll stick to apples."

After lunch, Henrietta took out her paste and scissors. Then she took out a poster she was working on. The poster showed the kinds of foods that are good for healthy, growing bodies. And right in the middle of the poster was a picture of a peanut butter and jam sandwich.

The picture reminded her of her sticky gloves.

It reminded her of hairy sandwiches.

It reminded her of the peanut butter and jam she could still smell on her gloves.

"Help!! I can't stand it!"

She took off her gloves. She picked up her scissors.

Snip! Off went one finger of her glove.

Snip! Off went a second.

Snip! Snip! Off went two more.

Henrietta looked at her gloves. She smelled them. She squeezed them.

"Well, that's that. No more smelly, sticky peanut butter and jam." Henrietta put the gloves back on. Now she had two thumbs and four fingers sticking out.

After school that day, Henrietta went to her violin lesson. "It's a very hot day for gloves, isn't it, Henrietta?" asked Mrs. Grundy.

"Yes, but I have this condition, and I must keep my hands covered, except for these four fingers and two thumbs." Henrietta held up her hands for Mrs. Grundy to see. "But don't worry, Mrs. Grundy. You won't notice any difference in my playing."

Henrietta picked up her violin and tucked it under her chin. Then she picked up her bow and began to play.

She squeaked.

She squawked.

She squealed.

She screeched.

When Henrietta finished, she carefully laid her violin and bow back in the case. She turned to Mrs. Grundy and smiled.

"There. You see? You couldn't notice any difference, could you?"

Mrs. Grundy didn't answer.

"You couldn't, could you, Mrs. Grundy?" Henrietta repeated.

Mrs. Grundy still didn't answer.

Henrietta looked closely at her teacher. "Mrs. Grundy. Are you okay? You look kinda' sick."

"I'm s-s-sure I'll be all right, Henrietta.

It's j-j-just that my ears are r-r-ringing, and I do feel a bit sh-sh-shaky."

Henrietta frowned. "Do you think it was my gloves, Mrs. Grundy?"

"If only it were- uh- yes, perhaps so." Mrs. Grundy wasn't looking quite as sick now that Henrietta had stopped playing. "Listen, Henrietta. I have a suggestion. I think you should stop coming for lessons while you have to wear gloves. Then, when your condition is cured, we'll start again...maybe."

* * *

When Henrietta went to bed that night, she was still wearing what was left of her gloves. She thought about all the things that had happened to her since she'd put them on. She'd spilt juice, dropped peas, broken dishes, scattered art paper, licked hairy sandwiches, and murdered Mozart.

"This is ridiculous," Henrietta muttered. She yanked off both gloves and flung them on the floor. "And besides, they still smell like peanut butter and jam."

Henrietta rummaged around in her drawer and found the list. She added a new line.

41

Henrietta stuffed the list back in her drawer, mumbled something about "who wants dumb ol' fingernails anyway", bit her nails, and fell sound asleep.

Now the list read:

How To Stop Biting Nails
      by Henrietta Lawes
1. Glammer Nails (too expensive)
2. Hypnosis (doesn't work)
3. NO FAIL NAILS (Hot stuff!!!)
   NO FAIL NAILS (failed - not hot enough)
4. Gloves (the answer??)
   Gloves (not the answer)
5. ???

Nailbiters Unite!

No one in the Lawes family mentioned Henrietta's gloves or Henrietta's nails at breakfast the next morning. Not even Hank. But when Henrietta got to school, *everybody* wanted to know why she wasn't wearing her gloves. Especially, dear sweet Kate.

"What? No gloves today, Henrietta?" Kate smarmed. "What about your so-called condition?"

"My gloves and my condition are *my* business," snarled Henrietta. "And I'll thank you to keep your nose out!"

"Ooohhh. Aren't we touchy today?"

Henrietta's eyes narrowed.

Henrietta's lips tightened.

Henrietta's hands curled...into fists! "Perhaps you'd like to *feel* just how touchy we are, Kate."

"C'mere, Henrietta," yelled Natalie,

just in time to save Kate from the fate of a Henrietta-sized fist sandwich.

"Boy, that Kate makes me mad!" Henrietta fumed.

"Don't pay any attention to her," soothed Sophie. "Getting you mad is just what she wants. And like a dummy, you always fall for it."

Henrietta looked disgusted with herself. "Yeh, I suppose you're right. But I don't want her to *ever* find out why I was wearing gloves."

"Well, if you tell us, we'll never tell, will we?" said Laura, looking first at Sophie and then at Natalie.

"Never."

"Never."

Henrietta studied Laura's face.

Henrietta studied Sophie's face.

Henrietta studied Natalie's face.

"Okay," Henrietta smiled. "You're my three best friends, and I can trust you. Look!" She held out her hands with her fingers spread wide.

Sophie, Laura and Natalie all looked at Henrietta's hands.

"I don't see any...condition," said Sophie.

"Neither do I," said Laura.

"Me neither," said Natalie.

"It's my fingernails!" hissed Henrietta. "Look at 'em. You can't even see 'em, can you? That's 'cause they're not there."

"Is that all?" asked Laura.

"What d'you mean 'is that all'," yelled Henrietta. "I've got to stop biting them. I bite 'em everyday. I bite 'em every night. I bite 'em for breakfast. I bite 'em for lunch. I bite 'em for dinner. Isn't that enough? That's why I wore gloves — so I wouldn't be able to. But it didn't work. Gloves made me do everything wrong. I spilt juice and peas and paper. I broke dishes. I murdered Mozart. And, worst of all, I ate hairy sandwiches!"

"Hairy sandwiches?" repeated Laura, Sophie and Natalie all together. "Ooooo-hhhh, yuk!"

"Yuk is right!" Henrietta agreed. "So what am I going to do now? I just gotta stop biting my nails."

"Well, so have I."

"Me too."

"And me."

Henrietta's eyes opened wide. Her jaw dropped. "What?" she gasped. "Do you mean . . . do you mean . . . you . . ." She looked at each of her three friends. "You all...you *all*... bite your nails too?"

"Yep."

"Yep."

"Yep."

Henrietta smiled. Then she started to laugh. She laughed harder. She threw her head back and laughed even harder. Sophie, Laura and Natalie started to laugh, too. They laughed harder and harder. The four girls held their stomachs. They collapsed in their chairs. Tears ran down their faces.

Soon everyone in the classroom was

looking at them. Some of the other children started to laugh too, just because Henrietta and her three friends looked so funny laughing so hard. Even Kate laughed.

The laughter didn't stop until Mrs. Hayford tapped her ruler on the desk and said, "All right everyone, it's time to settle down and take out your history books. Today we're studying the American Civil War."

Henrietta, Sophie, Laura and Natalie wiped their teary cheeks with the backs of their hands and took out their books. Every few minutes a little giggle escaped from one of them while Mrs. Hayford talked about the War.

"The American Civil War was the war in which people from the northern states of the United States joined together to get rid of slavery. One or two people from the northern states couldn't have stopped slavery by themselves, but lots of people united in a common cause were able to."

Henrietta raised her hand. "Do you mean if people unite they can do things easier than if they try to do it alone?"

"That's right, Henrietta," said Mrs. Hayford.

"So if one person is having trouble doing something alone, someone else can help, and then it won't be so hard for that one person. Right?"

"That's right, Henrietta."

Henrietta didn't ask any more questions during the history lesson, but when she and Laura and Sophie and Natalie walked home from school that afternoon, she said, "I've been thinking a lot about what Mrs. Hayford said. Especially the part about uniting."

"Yeah, I liked that bit, too," agreed Sophie.

"Well, I've got an idea. I can't stop biting my nails. Neither can you." Henrietta looked at her three friends. They each nodded. "I've tried to stop biting my nails by myself, but I can't. Neither can you. So how about if we unite and help each other?"

"Great idea!"

"Super!"

"Fantastic!"

"How about if we start a club?" Henrietta continued. "A club of nailbiters."

"Fantastic!"

"Super!"

"Great idea!"

48

"And how about if we call the club...
Nailbiters United?"

"Wow! That's a great name, Henrietta!
When's our first meeting? Where can we
meet?"

"How about tomorrow, after school, in
my bedroom. And we'll try to think of
ways to help each other stop chewing our
nails."

That night Henrietta found the list she'd scrunched up in the back of her drawer. She smoothed out the wrinkles, crossed out the question marks beside number five, and wrote, "Nailbiters United". The list now looked like this:

How To Stop Biting Nails
by Henrietta Lawes
1. Glammer Nails (too expensive)
2. Hypnosis (doesn't work)
3. NO FAIL NAILS (Hot stuff!!!)
   NO FAIL NAILS (failed - not hot enough)
4. Gloves (the answer??)
   Gloves (not the answer)
5. ??? Nailbiters United

Henrietta turned off her light and snuggled under the covers. She was so excited about Nailbiters United that she forgot all about biting her nails. In two minutes she fell sound asleep.

We Can Do It

"Natalie, Sophie and Laura are coming over after school today," Henrietta announced the next morning.

"That's nice," said Mrs. Lawes. "I have a meeting this afternoon, so if I'm not home, you can help yourselves to some carrot cake."

"Thanks, Mom. We're having a meeting too. In my bedroom. We're starting a new club."

Hank, who had been reading the cornflakes box and paying no attention to the conversation between Henrietta and her mother, suddenly raised his head over the top of the box. "Club? What kinda' club?"

Henrietta looked at her brother.

She remembered how he'd made fun of her gloves.

She remembered how he'd made fun of

51

her NO FAIL NAILS nail polish.

She remembered how he'd made fun of hypnosis and how *he'd* fallen asleep!

"None of your business, Hank. It's a secret club, and I'll thank you to stay far away from my bedroom this afternoon."

"Awwww, that's not fair! Mom, make Henrietta tell me what kinda' club it is."

"I can't do that, Hank. How would you like it if I made you tell Henrietta about a secret club you were in?"

Hank didn't answer. He narrowed his eyes and glared at his sister.

"Well, Hank?"

Hank never answered, and all the way to school he mumbled and grumbled and muttered and spluttered about *unfair...* *stupid secret club...*and *dumb ol' girls.*

Sophie, Laura and Natalie were huddled together whispering in the back of the classroom when Henrietta walked in. "Hi! Whatcha' doin'?" asked Henrietta.

"Guess what!" Sophie exclaimed. "We've each thought of a way to make us stop biting our nails."

"Yeah! Listen to this..." began Laura.

"Shhhhhh!" Henrietta whispered. "Not now! Someone might hear us! Wait until after school."

All day long the four girls exchanged secret looks and secret smiles. No one noticed, except Kate. And it was driving Kate crazy. "What are you four smiling about?" she finally asked Henrietta.

"Why, Kate, I don't know what you mean," said Henrietta, putting on her biggest, cheesiest smile.

Kate glared at Henrietta. She glared at Laura and Natalie and Sophie. Laura and Natalie and Sophie put on their biggest, cheesiest smiles too.

"You *all* know perfectly well what I mean!" snarled Kate storming out of the classroom.

"Tsk, tsk. Temper, temper," Sophie chided.

"She may have a temper, but she's got something else too. Did anyone notice her nails?"

"No. What about them, Henrietta?"

"They're *perfect*! Absolutely perfect! All ten of 'em!"

"Revolting," said Natalie.

"Sickening," said Laura.

"Disgusting," said Sophie.

The moment school was out, the four nailbiters were off to Henrietta's house. They stopped in the kitchen long enough to grab the carrot cake, then scrambled up the stairs to Henrietta's room.

Stuck to her door was a large sign:

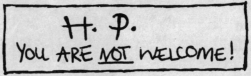

"That's for Hanky Panky," smiled Henrietta. "He'll probably try to stick his nosy-parker in here during our meeting."

"Brothers!" sneered Sophie. "They're nothing but trouble!"

54

Henrietta put the carrot cake on the floor, and the four girls sat in a circle around it. Each one sank her teeth into a piece of cake. "Now," said Henrietta with her mouth still full, "Nailbiters United can begin. Who has the first idea?"

Laura's hand shot up as though she was answering one of Mrs. Hayford's questions in class. "Can I start?"

"This isn't school, Laura," said Sophie.

"Oh, I forgot," said Laura looking a little embarrassed. "Anyway, here's my idea. Every time you start to bite- *STOP!* ...and call one of the other club members on the phone. You can't bite your nails and hold the phone at the same time."

"What about the hand that's not holding the phone?" interrupted Sophie.

"Sit on it."

"Oh. And what do you say to the person who's calling?"

"I've thought about that too. Here's what you say." Laura pulled a piece of paper from her pocket and read:

NAILBITERS UNITED PLEDGE
You want to bite your nails? Well don't!
We're Nailbiters United. we won't!

55

"That's great!" said Henrietta. "I think we should all copy it down so we won't forget."

"No need for that. I've already done it." Laura reached into her pocket again, took out three copies of the Nailbiters United Pledge, and gave one to each of the others.

"I want to tell my idea next," said Sophie.

"I'm after you," Natalie added quickly.

"My idea is for us to mark each others' nails."

Natalie looked puzzled. "You mean, write on each others' nails?"

"No, silly, not that kind of mark. I mean *mark*, like...give a grade. Like on a test."

"Oh."

Sophie went on with her explanation. "Here's the grades you can get. If your nails are all bitten-off, you get a one. That's the worst. If they're growing a little bit, you get a three or a four. If they're looking quite good, maybe a seven or an eight. If they're nearly perfect, you get a nine. And if they're all grown out, it's a ten!"

"That's like Dad's idea!" exclaimed

Henrietta looking down at her chewed, jagged nails. "But I never got past three."

"That's *before* Nailbiters United," Sophie reminded her. "It's different now. We're here to help you. And help each other . . ."

"I'd like to help myself to some carrot cake!" Hank's head poked in the door.

"Hank!" yelled Henrietta. "Can't you read? The sign says, *You are not welcome!* Now buzz off, Buster!"

"Not without my share of cake." Hank stuck his foot in the door. He smiled a big, cheesy smile. "I adopt the motion that Hank gets a piece of cake. All in favour —"

"I wish someone would adopt *you!*" snarled Henrietta. She handed Hank the cake and slammed the door shut. She collapsed against it and heaved a heavy sigh. "Is it any wonder I bite my nails when I have to put up with that...that ...*toad!*"

"Poor Henrietta."

"I see why you have to be tough."

"What a creep Hank is! Now let's get back to my idea," Sophie suggested. "What do you think?"

"We think it's great, and we think we should do it," said Henrietta. "Right, everyone?"

"Right!"

Sophie smiled. Out of her pocket she pulled a sheet of paper. Along the top was written the names of the four nail-biters. Down the left side was a space for dates. "This is our marking sheet. Each time we rate our nails, we'll write down the mark we got for that day. Let's start today."

"Do we *have* to?" Henrietta hid her hands between her legs.

Sophie looked Henrietta straight in the eye. "Out with your hands, Henrietta. This is serious business!"

The club members agreed on the following marks for May the 2nd.

Sophie – 2
Laura – 2
Natalie – 3
Henrietta – 1

"Now *my* idea," said Natalie. She reached into her pocket and pulled out a tin Band-aid box. She shook it to show it was empty. "Every time somebody bites their nails, it'll cost them 5 pence. We'll keep the money in this box, and whoever gets ten out of ten first, gets to keep the money...and the box!"

"When do we put the money in?"

"Each time we rate our nails. And since we've just rated them — and we've all been biting them — I think we should each put in 5 pence right now. And I'll be the first." Clunk!

"Agreed." Clunk!

"Right." Clunk!

"OK." Clunk!

Natalie shook the tin again. "Let's make that our first and last payment, Nailbiters." Then she turned to Henrietta. "Now what's your idea, Henrietta?"

Henrietta sighed heavily. She looked down at her nails. She looked up at each of her three friends. "I don't have an idea. I've already tried all my ideas and none of 'em worked. Not one."

The three friends smiled at her. "Don't worry, Henrietta. Nailbiters United will get you through."

* * *

Just as Henrietta was about to crawl into bed that night, the phone rang. "It's for you, Henrietta," yelled her mother. "It's Sophie. She says it's an emergency. Something about tooth and nail..."

Henrietta raced to the phone. "Hi, Sophie..."

"Quick, Henrietta! The pledge. I'm about to bite..."

"Sit on your other hand. Now repeat after me:

You want to bite your nails? Well, *don't!*
We're Nailbiters United. We *won't!*"

Sophie repeated the pledge. She repeated it again. Then she let out a deep breath. "Thanks Henrietta. I think I'm okay now. See you tomorrow."

Henrietta went back to her room and took out the list. She added number 6 and beside it she wrote, NU (short for Nailbiters United) — *We can do it.*

Now the list said:

How To Stop Biting Nails
     by Henrietta Lawes
1. Glammer Nails (too expensive)
2. Hypnosis (doesn't work)
3. NO FAIL NAILS (Hot stuff!!!)
   NO FAIL NAILS (failed - not hot
enough)
4. Gloves (the answer??)
   Gloves (not the answer)
5. ??? Nailbiters United
6. NU - We can do it!

Henrietta crawled into bed. She took one last look at her nails before turning out the light. "I can't *afford* to bite my nails anymore. And besides, I wanna' be the first to get ten out of ten."

That night Henrietta dreamed she wore ten shiny silver rings, one on each finger.

Can We Do It?

"Having another one of your silly club meetings today, girls?"

Hank followed the four nailbiters up the stairs and past Henrietta's room. "And you can take that dumb note off your dumb door too, Henrietta," he called back over his shoulder." I wouldn't come into your rotten bedroom for anything!"

"Oh no, Hank? Not even for a big, fat piece of gooey chocolate cake with gooey chocolate icing? You wouldn't come in even for that, Hanky Panky?" Henrietta leaned against her bedroom door and licked the ends of each of her fingers.

Hank jerked to a stop. He turned around and slowly started walking back toward his sister. "Henrietta! If you've taken the whole cake again and not left any for me, you're in big trouble, understand? Now give me some cake!"

Henrietta giggled. "Oh Hank. You're so gubbalul!"

"Gubbalul?"

"Yes, Hank. Gubbalul."

"Do you by any chance mean 'gullible', Henrietta? Gull-a-bul. Read my lips." Hank pointed to his mouth. "And don't use words you don't know the meaning of, Henrietta. Now where's my cake?"

"I happen to know the meaning of gubbalul, Hank. It means you! You fall for anything. If you don't believe *me* about the chocolate cake, Hank, why don't you go downstairs and see for yourself."

Hank charged past Henrietta, down the stairs to check out the chocolate cake. Henrietta closed her bedroom door and cymbal-slapped her hands together. "Well that takes care of him for a little while. Boy, I wish we *did* have some chocolate cake!"

"Forget cake, Henrietta," said Natalie in her best tough-guy accent. "We're talkin' nails." She took the Band-aid box out of her pocket and shook it. "We're also talkin' money. This ol' box is gettin' heavy, girls, and that means just one thing. There's been a whole lotta' nail-bitin' goin' on."

"I can tell you *exactly* how much biting's been going on," said Sophie. She unfolded the list with the nailbiters' names written along the top. "Hmmmm. Let's see. At our last meeting, Natalie got the highest mark. Seven. Henrietta, you were five." Natalie ran her finger down the row of numbers under Henrietta's name. "You had a six one week and then the next week you were back down to three. What happened?"

Henrietta looked disgusted. "That was the week of the relay race. I got so nervous before the race, I bit my nails off."

"Well, that was pretty dumb," said Laura. "You *won!*"

"Yeah, but I didn't know we were going to win *before* I bit 'em, did I? Anyway, I've got 'em back up to five now. I'm half-way there."

Sophie continued reading the numbers on the list. "Laura, you got an eight once. Now you're at five too."

Laura moaned. "You can blame that on the beetles."

"The Beatles? I thought you loved the Beatles. You've got all their records!"

"Not *those* Beatles. Real beetles. Bugs. Creepy crawlies. I had to give my report on beetles in class, and I *hate* standing up in front of everyone. So, I had a little nibble to calm my nerves."

"Some nibble," said Natalie. "You nibbled off three marks. And it cost you fifteen pence." She shook the Band-aid box.

"That's okay, Laura. You'll get back up to eight in no time." Sophie looked down at her own nails. "You'll probably even get to eight before I do. I haven't made it past six yet. I think mine grow slower than everyone elses."

"They don't grow *slower*, Sophie, you bite *faster!*" Henrietta laughed. "Now let's count up and see how much money we've got."

Natalie opened the Band-aid box and dumped the money out on the floor. A tightly folded piece of paper dropped out of the box too. Natalie unfolded it. "I've been keeping track of how much everyone's paid." She read down the list.

Laura 15 pence
Sophie 20 pence
Natalie 10 pence
Henrietta 20 pence

Natalie added up the numbers. "Sixty-five pence total," she said.

"Wow! Laura yelled. "That means that, right now, for my fifteen pence, I could get back sixty-five! Right?"

"Of course, right!" Henrietta answered, slightly impatiently. "That's what it's all about. That's the incentive."

"The what?" asked the three other nailbiters in unison.

"The incentive. A good reason to do something, or not to do something. That's what an incentive is."

"You mean, it's an incentive for me to get ten out of ten before the rest of you do because then I would get the money?" Natalie asked.

"Yep. My big incentive is to get the silver ring Dad promised me if I stopped biting my nails." Henrietta paused a minute. Then she smiled. "'Course it would be nice if I got the money too!"

"Well, none of us is going to get anything if we don't stop nibbling," Laura muttered. Then she added, "I think we should each put in another five pence – just to make a little better incentive."

The four nailbiters each dropped another five pence into the Band-aid box. Then, as they'd done after every meeting, they clasped hands and, all together, repeated the Nailbiters United Pledge.

"You want to bite your nails? Well, *don't!* We're Nailbiters United. We *won't!*"

That night Henrietta pulled the list out of her drawer and quickly read down through it. "I've gotta' hand it to ya', Henrietta," she said quietly to herself, "You've got guts. You may not have Glamour Nails, Kid, but you've got guts."

She added number seven and beside it wrote, NU...*Can* we do it? The list now looked like this:

```
How To Stop Biting Nails
    by Henrietta Lawes
1. Glammer Nails (too expensive)
2. Hypnosis (doesn't work)
3. NO FAIL NAILS (Hot stuff!!!)
   NO FAIL NAILS (failed - not hot
   enough)
4. Gloves (the answer??)
   Gloves (not the answer)
5. ??? Nailbiters United
6. NU - We can do it!
7. NU - can we do it?
```

Henrietta turned off her light, snuggled deep down in her bed and sighed a heavy sigh. "Wish there was such a thing as a magic wand," she thought as she closed her eyes and dropped off to sleep.

A New Member?

Henrietta carefully folded four paper napkins and placed one beside each plate. She looked at the kitchen clock. Only two minutes had passed since the last time she looked.

"Mom, how much longer do we have to wait for Dad? I'm starving!"

"Me too," Hank added.

Mrs. Lawes stopped slicing tomatoes. "Look, you two, stop nagging. To hear you, anyone would think you hadn't eaten in weeks. Dad's probably having to wait. You know what it can be like at the dentist."

"Did he have toothache?" asked Henrietta.

"No, he's just having a check-up."

"Well, if he doesn't get here pretty soon, I might faint from hunger." Henrietta flopped into a chair and wiped her forehead with the back of her hand.

"Spare us, Henrietta," Hank muttered. "You think you're a princess or something?"

Hank's remark made Henrietta forget about the possibility of fainting from hunger.

His remark made Henrietta forget about her growling stomach.

But his remark made Henrietta *remember* her hot temper.

Slowly Henrietta pulled herself up out of her chair and swaggered over to Hank. "I'll princess you, Hank. I'll —"

"Whoa. Hold on there." Their father stood at the kitchen door. "What's this I hear about a princess?" He tossed his jacket onto a chair, walked over to Hank and Henrietta, and clamped his hands firmly on top of their heads. Hank and Henrietta had no choice but to stand and stare at each other, nose to nose.

The sight of her son and daughter locked under their father's grip tickled Mrs. Lawes so much that she burst out laughing. "What you have in your hands, Dear, is a starving prince and princess. They haven't eaten a thing since school except two sandwiches, eight cookies and a quart of juice. Their little tummies are growling for food and their little tempers are *HOT!*"

"Well, let's eat then! I'm hungry too!" Mr. Lawes released Hank and Henrietta's heads. Then he opened his mouth wide and pointed inside. "Look, Kids! No cavities!"

Hank and Henrietta glanced at each other, clicked their tongues in disgust, and turned away from their father.

"No look, no eat," teased Mr. Lawes, still pointing.

"Awwww Dad. I don't want to look at your dumb teeth," protested Hank.

"C'mom, Dad...," began Henrietta.

"No look, no eat," repeated Mr. Lawes who was having a hard time keeping his mouth wide open without laughing.

"Better do as he says if you want to eat," laughed Mrs. Lawes.

"It's not fair," Hank muttered as he quickly glanced into his father's gaping mouth.

"Other parents don't do this to their kids," Henrietta muttered as she quickly glanced in there too.

Mr. Lawes closed his mouth. He hugged Hank. He hugged Henrietta. He kissed Mrs. Lawes. "Boy! I'm really starving now! Let's eat! By the way, Henrietta, what's this about a princess?"

"Nothing. Hank just said I acted like one."

"Well, it reminds me of something I read in a magazine at the dentist's office."

"Oh yeah? What kinda' magazine?" asked Henrietta.

Before Mr. Lawes could answer, Mrs. Lawes asked, "You weren't reading one of those 'ladies' magazines, were you, Dear?"

Mr. Lawes cleared his throat. "Well, the cover said something about prize-winning tomatoes, so naturally..."

"We understand, Dad," grinned Henrietta, winking at her mother. "But, Dad, *I'm* not interested in tomatoes."

"But you *are* interested in nailbiting, aren't you?" he asked.

"So? What about it? Does it tell you how to stop?"

"Well, not exactly. But guess who's also a nailbiter?"

"Who?" asked Henrietta. "Somebody famous?"

"Very."

Henrietta thought, but she couldn't think of anyone. "C'mon Dad, who is it?"

"Would you believe...The Princess of Wales!"

Henrietta's chin dropped, and her eyes popped. "You mean, Princess Diana? The one who lives in the Palace? The one who married Prince Charles? *That* Princess?"

"The very same."

Henrietta folded her arms across her chest and flopped back into her chair. "Wait'll I tell the club about this!"

"What club, Henrietta?" asked Hank.

But before Henrietta had time to say, "None of your business, Hank," Hank had already guessed. "So *that's* what you four have been up to. You're a bunch of nailbiters!"

Henrietta didn't say a word.

She looked at Hank.

She looked at her mother.

She looked at her father.

Mr. Lawes put down his knife and fork. He looked straight at Hank. "Hank," he said, "I don't think I *need* to say this, but I'm going to anyway. Henrietta's club is Henrietta's business. If *she* wants to tell anyone about it, *she* can. *You* can't. Right?"

Hank didn't say a word.

He looked at Henrietta.

He looked at his mother.

He looked at his father.

Finally Hank spoke just one word. "Right," he said.

After dinner Henrietta phoned the other three nailbiters and called an emergency meeting. Same time. Same place.

The next afternoon Sophie, Natalie and Laura sat cross-legged on Henrietta's bedroom floor.

"What *is* it, Henrietta?"

"C'mon, Henrietta, tell us."

"Don't keep us waiting, Henrietta."

Henrietta closed the door. Without saying a word, she went over to her dressing table, took out a pad of paper and a pencil, and sat down on the floor with the other nailbiters.

"Well," began Henrietta, "I think we should invite a new member to join Nailbiters United."

"What!"

"Who?"

"Why?"

"Because," Henrietta continued, "she may be able to help us, and we may be able to help her."

"Who?" Laura asked. "Who are you talking about?"

"I'm talking about Princess Diana, that's who. *The* Princess Diana. I think she's a nailbiter too! Well, it said so in the magazine."

Three chins dropped and six eyes popped.

"C'mon," said Henrietta impatiently, "Whadda' ya say? I think we should write today and ask her to join Nailbiters United."

Sophie looked puzzled. "You mean... just like that? Write to a princess...just like that?"

"Yeah. Why not?" Henrietta flipped open the pad of paper. Sophie, Laura and Natalie all looked at each other.

"Well?" demanded Henrietta.

They looked back at Henrietta. "Well, why not?" they all agreed.

"Right," said Henrietta. "Now, how do we start the letter? Do we say, 'Dear Diana'?"

Laura shook her head. "I don't think you just say 'Dear Diana' to a princess. I think you have to say something like, 'Dear Your Royal Majesty'."

"That's to the Queen, not the princess," Sophie said with a tone of authority that the other nailbiters didn't dare argue with. "I think we should say, 'Dear Lady Diana'."

"That sounds too old," Natalie protested. "How about 'Dear Mrs. Prince Charles'?"

"Dear Mrs. Prince Charles! Yuk! That sounds terrible!" Henrietta fell over backwards, clutching her throat, pretending she was about to be sick. "You don't call a princess 'Mrs.' even if she is married!"

Henrietta sat back up again. "I think we should just say, 'Dear Princess Diana'."

Natalie, Sophie and Laura finally agreed that 'Dear Princess Diana' sounded best, and Henrietta, in her very neatest handwriting, was voted to write the letter for the club. Here's what it said:

Dear Princess Diana,

We are writing to you because we have a problem. We bite our nails. We bite them all the time. We just can't stop.

We read in a magazine that you bite your nails too. If you have stopped biting your nails, would you PLEASE tell us how you did it?

If you haven't stopped biting your nails, would you like to join our new club? It's called Nailbiters United and we help each other not bite our nails.

Would you like to be a member? We each pay five pence each time we bite our nails, but you don't have to. For you, it's free.

yours sincerely,
Henrietta Lawes
Sophie Baird   Laura James
Natalie Pierce

Henrietta carefully folded the letter and tucked it into an envelope. "Do you think it will get there if I just put Buckingham Palace, London? No street number or anything?"

"'Course," said Laura. "Everyone knows where Buckingham Palace is. When I wrote to Santa at the North Pole, he got it, and they don't even have roads there!"

"Laura!" snapped Sophie. "Don't be stupid. This is serious business."

Henrietta licked the envelope. Then she wrote her own address on the back. "This gets sent first thing tomorrow morning. Meeting adjourned."

* * *

That night when Henrietta pulled her list out of the drawer, it ripped into two pieces. "Darn," she muttered. "Now I'll have to copy it all over."

She took out the pad of paper she'd used to write to the Princess. "Oh well," thought Henrietta. "The Princess will probably ask to see my list anyway, so I may as well make a new copy."

Henrietta's new wrinkle-free, smudge-free, tear-free list now looked like this:

How To Stop Biting Nails
by Henrietta Lawes
1. Glammer Nails (too expensive)
2. Hypnosis (doesn't work)
3. NO FAIL NAILS (Hot stuff!!!)
   NO FAIL NAILS (failed - not hot enough)
4. Gloves (the answer??)
   Gloves (not the answer)
5. ??? Nailbiters United
6. NU - We can do it!
7. NU - can we do it?
8. NU - A new member?

Henrietta slipped the new list between the pages of her *Believe it or Not* book so it wouldn't get wrinkled...just in case. She glanced at the envelope addressed to the Princess lying on her dressing table. "Maybe Buckingham Palace does need a street address," she thought as she turned off her light, pulled the covers up tightly under her chin and fell fast-asleep.

Ladies-in-Waiting

The next morning Henrietta dressed quickly, grabbed the envelope from her dressing table, and raced downstairs to breakfast.

"Will you post this for me today, Dad? It's very important. In fact, it's urgent. It's a matter of..."

"Hey! Hold on a minute." Mr. Lawes raised both hands, stick-'em-up-cowboy style. "How about a 'Good Morning, Father. And did you sleep well, Father?' before you start with the orders, bossy madam."

"Sorry, Dad," Henrietta gave her father a quick peck on the cheek.

"That's a bit better," he smiled. "I'll let you get away with it *this* time. Now what's this urgent letter all about?" He picked up the envelope and read the address. "Hmmmm. Well, well, well.

This wouldn't have anything to do with nailbiting by any chance, would it, Henrietta?"

"Yep! We've invited Princess Diana to join our club. For free!"

"You've what?" bellowed Hank from behind the cereal box. "You've invited the Princess to join your dumb club? Bet she won't even answer your dumb letter."

"Bet she will!"

"Bet she won't!"

"Will!"

"Won't!"

"Hank! Zip up!" ordered Mr. Lawes.

Hank zipped. His head disappeared behind the cereal box.

"Now," said Mr. Lawes turning back to Henrietta, "I'd be happy to post your letter to the Princess. I think it's a great idea."

"Do you think she'll join?"

"Don't know, but you can't lose anything by asking."

"Dad, how long will we have to wait for an answer?"

"Who knows? She must be very busy, and she probably gets hundreds of invitations every day. You'll just have to wait and see."

That afternoon at the Nailbiters United meeting, Henrietta reported on the posting of the letter. Then the four club members marked each other's nails. The marks were:

Sophie – 8
Laura – 9
Natalie – 7
Henrietta – 7

The week before, Natalie and Henrietta both had eights. But now they'd chewed their nails back down to sevens.

Natalie shook the Band-aid box. "Guess that means we pay up," she said to Henrietta.

Henrietta reached into her pocket and pulled out five pence. She cupped the money in her hands like a gambler with a pair of dice. "Come on, Princess Diana. Bring me some luck. I can't afford this much longer."

"When do you think she'll write back?"

"Dunno. Dad said it could take a long time."

But it didn't take a long time. By the time Nailbiters United next met, the Princess had written back to them. Henrietta waited until they were all settled on the floor in her bedroom before showing them the envelope. Each one studied it carefully.

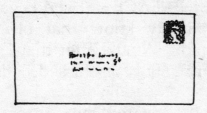

"Look at the stamp in the corner," Sophie pointed out. "It's got a crown in the middle."

"And the letters, 'ER'. Wonder what they stand for."

"Probably 'Ever Royal' or something like that," Natalie suggested. "But forget the envelope. Let's see what the letter says."

V-e-r-y carefully Henrietta tore open the envelope and took out the letter. At the top was a red crown with three feathers. Underneath, also in bright red, were the words BUCKINGHAM PALACE. Henrietta ran her finger across the crown and the words. "You can feel 'em!"

Sophie, Laura and Natalie each ran their fingers across the paper. "Wow! That *is* fancy!"

"Well, should I read it?"

"Yeah! Go ahead!"

Henrietta pulled herself up very straight and cleared her throat. "BUCK-INGHAM PALACE —" she began.

"We already know that bit," Laura interrupted. "What's after that?"

"Shhhh!" Sophie hissed. "Let her read!"

Henrietta cleared her throat again. "Ahem." Then she began to read.

> From: Lady-in-waiting to H.R.H.
> The Princess of Wales
> Dear Henrietta, Sophie, Laura and Natalie, The Princess of Wales has asked me to thank you for your letter.

"Oooh, that sounds so nice," murmured Natalie.

"Shhh!" Sophie hissed again.

> As I am sure you will appreciate, owing to the large number of similar requests —

"Similar requests?" Natalie interrupted again. "Are there *other* Nailbiters United clubs?"

"That's not what it means." Henrietta put down the letter. "It means other clubs have invited her to join too."

"Darn!" Natalie muttered.

Henrietta started to read again.

> ...owing to the large number of similar requests received by her Royal Highness —

"See?" This time it was Laura. "She *is* called 'Royal Highness'...just like I said."

"You said, 'Your Royal Majesty'," corrected Sophie.

"Right! You did!" Henrietta agreed. "Now may I continue *without* interruption, please?"

> ...similar requests received by her Royal Highness every day, it is simply not possible for her to accede to them all.

"Accede? What's accede? Does that mean she joining or not?" Natalie snatched the letter from Henrietta. "Where does it say that?"

"There." Henrietta pointed to the word.

Natalie read the sentence out loud to herself. "Bet if we'd said how old we are, she wouldn't have used words like that." She handed the letter back to Henrietta.

Henrietta glared at Natalie. "Maybe we can tell what she means if I read the next bit. If I don't get interrupted again, that is." Henrietta read on.

I am sorry to have to send you this disappointing reply —

"That's what accede means," muttered Natalie. "It means No."

"Natalie!"

"Well, that's what it means, doesn't it?"

Henrietta kept on reading.

Nevertheless, The Princess was delighted to receive your letter and asks me to send you her sincere thanks and best wishes.

Henrietta put the letter on the floor. She looked at her friends.

"Well, that's it. She doesn't want to join Nailbiters United...so we've just got to do it on our own."

"Ahhh, I didn't think she would anyway, really."

"Me neither."

"Too many clubs have already asked her."

"I guess it was a long shot," added Henrietta. "Still, it woulda' been nice." She picked up the letter, folded it, and tucked it back in the envelope. Then, as they'd done after every other meeting, the four club members clasped hands and, all together, repeated the Nailbiters United Pledge.

"You want to bite your nails? Well, *don't!*
We're Nailbiters United. We *won't!"*

* * *

That night Henrietta took out her *Believe It or Not* book with the list tucked inside. She added number nine and beside it scribbled a few words. The list now looked like this:

How To Stop Biting Nails
by Henrietta Lawes
1. Glammer Nails (too expensive)
2. Hypnosis (doesn't work)
3. NO FAIL NAILS (Hot stuff!!!)
   NO FAIL NAILS (failed - not hot enough)
4. Gloves (the answer??)
   Gloves (not the answer)
5. ??? Nailbiters United
6. NU - We can do it!
7. NU - can we do it?
8. NU - A new member?
9. NU - We're on our own...

Henrietta looked at her nails. "Seven isn't *so* bad," she thought, "and I did get up to eight once. And besides, (and this thought made Henrietta grin a very satisfied grin) I still won the bet with Hank!"

Within two minutes, Henrietta Lawes was sleeping her way to a bright, new morning.

United We Stand

It was two weeks later at the breakfast table when Mr. Lawes suddenly remembered the letter. "Did you ever get a reply from The Princess of Wales?"

Henrietta shrugged her shoulders. "Uh huh. Well, it wasn't actually from Princess Diana herself. It was from her Lady-in-Waiting."

"Well, what did she say?"

"She said she was too busy to join our club."

Mr. Lawes reached over and squeezed Henrietta's shoulder. "Sorry, Honey."

"It's okay. Club's still going. In fact, we're meeting this afternoon. Probably Sophie or Laura will win the money-box today."

"Money-box?" Her father's question made Hank stop chewing his toast and look over at his sister.

"It's really just an old Band-aid box. We each put in five pence whenever we bite our nails." Henrietta looked down at her hands. "I bet I've put in the most. Whoever gets their nails all grown out first, gets to keep all the money...and the box."

"You mean, whoever gets ten out of ten first?" Mr. Lawes asked.

"Yep. And it won't be me," sighed Henrietta.

Mrs. Lawes sipped her coffee. "You've been trying so hard, Henrietta. How's it going?"

"Pretty good. I still bite...but not so bad. What I've done is, I've stopped biting all my nails but one. See?" Henrietta held out her hands and spread her fingers wide. She had nine medium-sized nails and one very bitten, very jagged, very short thumbnail. She quickly tucked the thumbnail under her hand.

"Henrietta, that's wonderful!" her mother said. "I'd say you've licked it!"

"Chewed it, more like it," mumbled Hank.

Mr. Lawes gave Hank another "zip up" look and said to Henrietta, "I agree, honey. You've made it!"

93

Henrietta shook her head. "No I haven't. Not really. I have to get ten outta' ten to win the money-box or..." She paused and turned to her father, "...or to get the silver ring."

Mr. Lawes raised his eyebrows and sucked in his breath. "I'm afraid that *was* our agreement, Henrietta. Ten out of ten. When did you say your club meets again?"

"Today, after school. In my bedroom."

Hank snickered. "With all that loot in the Band-aid box, Henrietta, do you want me to stand guard?"

Henrietta rose from her chair, leaned over the table, and eyeballed Hank. "I told you, Hank, that when my nails were all grown out, I'd have ten very dangerous weapons. Well, watch your step, Kiddo, 'cause now I've got nine!"

Hank pretended to tremble and slid down low in his chair so that only the hair on his head stuck up over the top of the table. "Oh no, Henrietta. Please, I beg you. Have mercy. Have mercy on your poor defenceless brother..."

You'll be late for school, Kids," warned Mrs. Lawes. She knew how quickly a Hank-and-Henrietta skirmish could turn

into a Hank-and-Henrietta battle. "Now, off you go, both of you!"

Sophie, Laura and Natalie were waiting for Henrietta in the schoolyard. "Meeting after school, Henrietta?" Sophie asked.

"Yep. If everyone wants to."

"I do," nodded Laura.

"Me too," agreed Natalie.

Henrietta dug a little hole in the ground with the toe of her shoe. Without looking up at her three friends she asked, "Is anyone thinking about what I'm thinking about?"

"If you're thinking about a money box, then I'm thinking about what you're thinking about," said Natalie.

"If you're thinking about ten out of ten, then I'm thinking about what you're thinking about," said Sophie.

"If you're thinking that maybe today's the day, then I'm thinking about what you're thinking about," said Laura.

Henrietta laughed. "Guess we're all thinking about the same thing, huh? Wish we didn't have to go to school — we could have our meeting right now!"

When the bell rang that afternoon, the four club members threw their books into their school bags and hurried to Henrietta's house. They each grabbed one of Mrs. Lawes' freshly-baked ginger cookies and scrambled up the stairs to Henrietta's room.

Sophie took out the marking sheet.

Natalie took out the Band-aid box.

Henrietta called the meeting to order. "Sophie, what marks did everyone get last time?"

Sophie ran her finger down the marking sheet and called out the number under each club member's name.

Sophie – 9
Laura – 9
Natalie – 7
Henrietta – 9

"Thank you, Sophie," said Henrietta. "Now...Nailbiters, spread your fingers!" Just as they had done in all their other meetings, Sophie, Laura, Natalie and Henrietta placed both hands on the floor in front of them and spread their fingers wide. Without a word, they all studied each other's nails.

Natalie spoke first. "I think Sophie still gets a nine because she has two nails that are a lot shorter than the rest. I think Henrietta still gets a nine too...because of her thumb." Natalie looked at her own hands. "Mine are okay on one hand, but my other hand is horrible. I guess I still get a seven."

Sophie and Henrietta agreed with Natalie's marks. "What about Laura? What do you give her?"

Natalie looked at Laura's nails. Then she looked up at Sophie and Henrietta. "To Laura..." she began slowly, "to Laura...I'd give the money box!"

A big, big grin spread over Laura's face.

"I'd give the money box to Laura too," agreed Henrietta.

"Me too," said Sophie. She picked up the marking sheet, and under Laura's name she wrote a great big number ten and drew lots of lines under it.

Natalie shook the Band-aid box and passed it to Laura. "Here, Laura, it's all yours."

Laura dumped the money on the floor and counted. One pound and eighty-five pence.

"Wow! What are you going to do with it?" asked Sophie.

"Well, I've been thinking about that for a long time, and I know exactly what I'm going to do."

"You do?"

"Yes I do. I'm going to buy the most beautiful, the most glamorous, the most elegant bottle of nail polish I can find, and at our next meeting, we can all paint our nails."

"Oh Laura, that's a great idea!" Natalie exclaimed.

"And that's not all," Laura continued. "If there's any money left over, I'll spend it on a big, fat bar of chocolate... split four ways!"

Sophie, Natalie, and Henrietta grinned at Laura. Then Henrietta quickly stood up, raised her fist and yelled, "Three cheers for Laura."

"Hip hip hooray!"
"Hip hip hooray!"
"Hip hip hooray!"

"Thanks," said Laura. "Now we'd better say the Pledge. Nailbiters United isn't over until we've all stopped biting our nails. Right?"

Sophie, Natalie and Laura stood up, and as they'd done after every other meeting, the four club members clasped hands and, all together, repeated the Nailbiters United Pledge.

"You want to bite your nails? Well, *don't!* We're Nailbiters United. *We won't!"*

* * *

That night Henrietta didn't look at her list. The last time she'd added number nine and beside it had written, "We're on our own." "Nothing new to add," she thought, "We're *still* on our own."

Henrietta reached under her pillow for her pyjamas. "Oooh!" She jerked her hand out quickly. "What's under my pillow?"

Slowly, carefully, Henrietta lifted the corner of her pillow. There lay the Band-aid box. Laura's Band-aid box. "She must have forgotten to take it. I'd better call her right now in case she thinks it's lost."

Henrietta raced down the stairs, nearly knocking her father over on his way up. "Hey! What's the hurry?"

"Laura won the Band-aid box today, and she forgot it. It's under my pillow. I'm going to call her..."

"Oh," said Mr. Lawes continuing on up the stairs. "Tell me what she says."

Two minutes later, Henrietta raced up the stairs, nearly knocking her father over on his way down. "What did Laura say?" he asked.

Henrietta looked puzzled. "She has her box, so I don't know what that one is doing under my pillow."

"Oh," said Mr. Lawes continuing on down the stairs. "That's curious."

Two minutes later, Henrietta raced down the stairs again, nearly knocking her father over on his way up. "Oh Dad," cried Henrietta, "It's *so* beautiful." She threw her arms around her father's waist and hugged as tightly as she could. "And it fits perfectly. Look!"

Henrietta held out her hand so that her father could see the shiny, silver ring. Then she looked up at him. "But what about our agreement, Dad? I didn't get ten outta' ten."

"Well, Honey, I look at it this way. You've earned that ring ten times over. Nine out of ten is good enough for me."

Henrietta sat down on the stairs and stared at her ring for a long, long time. "Wait'll I tell the club about this!"